I tip-toed over and peered through the small,
circular window in one of the hall doors. And
there they were, the entire school, pupils sitting
cross-legged on the floor, staff standing by the
piano. But Mrs Patel wasn't thumping away at
the ivories, and no hymns were being murdered.

Instead, every single person in the hall had
their hands up, and they were all staring in one
direction. I looked that way as well, and saw a
menacing, hooded figure . . . holding a gun!

I didn't have time to do anything. Suddenly
something hard and blunt was pressed into my
spine, and my blood ran cold. A female voice
hissed in my ear.

'Put your hands where I can see them, kid,'
it said. 'That way you might make it to
lunch-time . . .'

*Sam, the Girl Detective: The Great Rock
'n' Roll Ransom* is the fifth title in a series
of hilarious detective mysteries starring
Sam Marlowe, intrepid girl detective.

Also by Tony Bradman,
published by Yearling Books:

SAM, THE GIRL DETECTIVE

SAM, THE GIRL DETECTIVE:
THE CASH BOX CAPER

SAM, THE GIRL DETECTIVE:
THE CASE OF THE MISSING
MUMMY

SAM, THE GIRL DETECTIVE:
THE SECRET OF THE
SEVENTH CANDLE

published by Corgi Books:
A STACK OF STORY POEMS

The Great Rock 'n' Roll Ransom

TONY BRADMAN

Illustrated by Doffy Weir

YEARLING BOOKS

SAM, THE GIRL DETECTIVE:
THE GREAT ROCK 'N' ROLL RANSOM

A YEARLING BOOK : 0 440 863104

First publication in Great Britain

PRINTING HISTORY
Yearling edition published 1994

Set in 14/16pt Monotype Century Schoolbook by
Phoenix Typesetting, Ilkley, West Yorkshire.

Yearling Books are published by Transworld Publishers
Ltd, 61-63 Uxbridge Road, Ealing, London W5 5SA, in
Australia by Transworld Publishers (Australia) Pty.
Ltd, 15-25 Helles Avenue, Moorebank, NSW 2170, and
in New Zealand by Transworld Publishers (N.Z.) Ltd,
3 William Pickering Drive, Albany, Auckland.

Made and printed in Great Britain by
Cox & Wyman Ltd, Reading, Berks

FOR SUE COOK,
THE GREAT ROCK 'N' ROLL
EDITOR

Sam, the Girl Detective
THE GREAT ROCK 'N' ROLL
RANSOM

Chapter One

It was a crisp, beautiful, autumn morning, the kind that makes you realize how good it is to be alive and eleven years old and walking down a nice, quiet street like Hammett Avenue.

Actually, I should have been worried out of my mind.

I was late for school, and Mrs Sternwood, my teacher, has always been a pretty tough cookie where punctuality is concerned. Especially mine. I can't blame her. This would be the third time I'd missed registration in a week, and it *was* only Wednesday. If I kept it up I might even beat my own record.

So why was I strolling in the bright sunshine as if I didn't have a care in the world? Why was I scanning the pavements for the crispest leaves to crunch under foot, instead of hurrying like a good little schoolgirl? Why was I feeling cool, calm and collected as I made a left into Leonard Road?

For starters, I'm Sam Marlowe, girl detective, and I don't get rattled. That's probably the most important lesson you learn as a private eye. If you panic whenever there's a problem, you might as well pack it in and try something you *can* handle. Train spotting, for instance.

I also had everything under control. I knew I could sneak into my school, Chandler Street Junior, without being caught. I had the perfect plan. It was very simple.

But then the best plans always are.

Leonard Road is quite short. There's a shop at the other end, one of those mini-markets where you can buy anything, from a bag of sweets to a bar of soap. But I wasn't heading there. I stopped just before the corner, at a narrow gap between two houses. Numbers 23 and 25, to be precise.

I turned round to check I wasn't being followed. The coast was clear. The tree-lined street was emptier than a classroom at the weekend. I smiled, and stepped swiftly and silently into the shadowed opening.

I crept down a small alley. It led to a high wall that was almost completely overgrown. Most people wouldn't have given it a second glance. But I'm not most people. I'm an ace detective, and I see stuff nobody else does. Which is how come I knew about the hidden door . . . my secret entrance into school.

I had discovered it when I'd been on patrol in the summer holidays. I like to keep an eye on my territory, especially when I haven't got much else to do. For some reason, I had been strangely drawn to the alley in Leonard Road. I suppose it was just the instinct of a super-sleuth.

Anyway, as soon as I'd seen the wall, I'd decided to investigate a bit further. I had parted some of the creepers covering the crumbling bricks . . . and had been surprised to find an ancient wooden door with the paint flaking off, home to several huge snails and a horde of hairy spiders.

I had been more surprised to discover that it opened fairly easily, and positively amazed by what was on the other side. For the door had brought me to a second, even narrower alley. One that led directly into my school!

It hadn't taken me long to work everything out. My class had done a local history project last term. So I was aware that when the school was built, a wall had been put up to separate the grounds from the gardens of the houses in Leonard Road. The door had probably been some kind of rear safety exit.

Over the years the area between the main school and the wall had gradually been filled in with loads of buildings – some extra classrooms, a new toilet block, the bike sheds, a boiler house for the central heating, the caretaker's special store with its 'Keep Out – This Means You!' sign.

By the time I began my career as a pupil at Chandler Street, you couldn't see the wall at all. Which meant, of course, that the door had been forgotten. Until a certain genius of a detective had found it, and realized how useful it could be . . . And here I was again, opening it and squeezing through.

I pushed the door shut behind me as softly as I could. I was facing a modern wall, which I now knew to be the back of the bike sheds. I was in a dark, gloomy space just wide enough for one person. The ground beneath my feet was a deep carpet of decayed, dead leaves and stray pieces of rubbish.

I paused at the end of the alley to make sure my route was clear. From there I eased into the shadow of the boiler house, then dashed across to the doors of the main building. I could only have been visible for a few seconds. Once inside, I ducked into the first room on the right.

Phew, I thought. So far, so good. The hardest part of my plan had gone smoothly. From here on, it should be easy.

I was standing in the over-sized cupboard that passes for our school library. No-one uses it, mainly because it doesn't contain anything interesting. Most of the books are absolutely pathetic. They're older and tattier than my parents, and much, much more boring. *If* that's possible.

Mind you, I'd been in it a lot recently. A couple of weeks ago, our head, Mr Pinkerton, had asked for someone to take charge of it, and I'd raised my hand. Mrs Sternwood had been so startled she'd done this

terrific imitation of a goldfish –
bulging eyes, mouth gaping wide,
the whole bit.

Don't get the wrong idea. Mrs
Sternwood might not approve of my
taste in books – I go for detective
stories with loads of action and plenty
of corpses – but she knows I love
reading. No, what had shocked her
was actually seeing me volunteer for
extra work. I thought she was going
to faint.

Mr Pinkerton, however, had a
'Library Monitor' badge pinned on
my school sweatshirt faster than I
can handcuff a villain, which is saying something. Mrs Sternwood had
treated me to one of her I-Know-
You're-Up-To-Something looks, but
there was nothing she could do, even
if she *was* right.

It had dawned on me the library
would be a perfect alibi whenever I
needed to disappear. And if I was
late for registration, why, that was
simply because I'd come in early to

tidy the shelves and had got involved in what I was doing. Using my secret entrance guaranteed no-one could prove otherwise.

I glanced at my watch. All I had to do was wait a few minutes. Then the corridor outside would be filled with the familiar sound of mayhem as everyone was herded down to assembly, giving me the chance to slip in with the others. Mrs Sternwood would probably be too busy to make any fuss.

But it didn't happen that way.

I listened as the time for assembly came and went, with no sound of children stampeding, and no teachers bellowing. I was puzzled . . . and soon I was curious. I eased open the door and peeked out. The corridor was deserted, and a thick, heavy silence seemed to hang in the air.

Immediately the hairs prickled on the back of my neck. They always do that when I have a feeling that something isn't right. I decided I'd

The corridor was deserted, and a thick heavy silence seemed to hang in the air.

better find out what was going on. So I padded off down the corridor, every sense alert for clues.

I checked the classrooms as I went along. Each was empty. At last I came to the reception area and the main entrance. The door to the secretary's office is on the left. There's a large hot drinks dispenser to one side, but I could see the door was open. Mrs Brown wasn't at her desk, though, and beyond it, I saw that Mr Pinkerton wasn't in his office, either.

Curiouser and curiouser, I thought, swinging round to face the hall doors. And that's when I saw it – the enormous banner Class 7 had spent the last week preparing. It was strung from one corner of the ceiling to the other, and said in huge letters: *'CHANDLER STREET SCHOOL WELCOMES RIFF THUNDER!'*

Ah, yes, I should have remembered. Today was . . . The Big Day.

A new boy joined our class a few weeks ago. His name is Justin, and he's pretty much like anybody else, except that his dad happens to be Riff Thunder, leader of the legendary heavy metal band, The Rock Lords. Their latest single is called *Prisoner of Your Love*, and I hear it's racing up the charts. Don't quote me on that, though. The only prisoners *I'm* interested in are the villains I catch and send to jail.

It turned out that Mr Pinkerton is the Rock Lords' biggest fan, and our wonderful head had been trying to get Riff to visit the school ever since Justin had started. To Mr Pinkerton's delight, the star had finally agreed. He was due this morning, which accounted for the banner being in place.

What it didn't explain was where several hundred noisy children, one dozen assorted, harassed teachers, and one rather plump school secretary had vanished to.

I ran through some of the alternatives. A whole school project on the

Marie Celeste? A sudden, devastating plague? I know, I thought at last. I'll bet everybody had been sent straight into the hall as soon as they had arrived. The school had been bubbling with excitement yesterday, and that would be a typical teacher tactic for keeping the lid on us kids.

I tip-toed over and peered through the small, circular window in one of the hall doors. And there they were, the entire school, pupils sitting cross-legged on the floor, staff standing by the piano. But Mrs Patel wasn't thumping away at the ivories, and no hymns were being murdered.

Instead, every single person in the hall had their hands up, and they were all staring in one direction. I looked that way as well, and saw a menacing, hooded figure . . . holding a gun!

I didn't have time to do anything. Suddenly something hard and blunt was pressed into my spine, and my blood ran cold. A female voice hissed in my ear.

'Put your hands where I can see them, kid,' it said. 'That way you might make it to lunch-time . . .'

Chapter Two

I did exactly as I was told. Another lesson you learn as a private eye is not to disagree with any adult who's got a gun and a bad attitude. The person behind me had both, and apparently wasn't afraid to use either.

I was prodded through the hall doors, then given a shove that caught me off balance and almost sent me sprawling. I managed to stay on my feet, though, and most of the teachers protested. Mrs Sternwood stepped forward and put her arm round me.

'Quiet!' I heard another female voice yell. 'And stay where you are!' It must have been the hooded figure

I'd seen, I thought. Mrs Sternwood took no notice.

'Are you OK, Samantha?' she said.

'Thanks, Miss, I'm fine,' I said. 'At least, I think I am.'

Mrs Sternwood smiled, although that didn't stop her looking worried. I opened my mouth to ask what was occurring, but the question never made it past my teeth.

'Where did *she* come from?' I heard the hooded figure say, angrily. 'You were supposed to have rounded up *all* the blasted kids, dimwit. She could have blown the whole job.'

'I don't know, do I?' the first voice replied, just as crossly. 'Maybe she was hiding in a cupboard, or something. And how many times do I have to tell you not to call me a dimwit?'

I turned, and saw that the person who had sneaked up on me outside was dressed in exactly the same way as the figure I'd glimpsed through the door. Both were wearing black trainers, black jeans, black tracksuit

I didn't think this couple had come trick or treating

tops with hoods, and ghastly masks that hid their faces. One showed a vampire, the other a witch.

Halloween *was* only a few weeks away, but I didn't think this pair had come trick or treating. They were criminals, and I had walked into the middle of some sort of major scam. Not that they were getting on very well. They were arguing and trying to keep their voices down at the same time.

That's not easy. I should know. My big brother Philip and I do it constantly. Our parents hate it when we have a row.

'Er . . . sorry to butt in,' I said. 'Do I take it this means we're not having our usual assembly?'

Somebody giggled, but soon fell into silence as the masks of our captors swung in my direction. I didn't need X-ray vision to guess they weren't laughing behind the plastic.

'Well, well, our latecomer seems to be a bit of a *clever-clogs*,' said the vampire sarcastically. She made the word sound like the mess a dog with a bad stomach might leave on the pavement. 'And if there's one thing we can't stand, it's a child who thinks she's clever.'

'I'm with you there,' said the witch.

'Now what we think *you* should do . . .' said the vampire.

'Is sit down with everyone else and keep very, very . . . *quiet*,' continued the witch.

'Got it?' they chorused, loudly.

'You'd better do as they say,

Samantha,' murmured Mrs Sternwood, her gaze fixed on the villains.

'OK, Miss,' I said. *'You're* in charge.'

I wasn't going to leave them thinking they'd won. I turned on my heel and sauntered off, the way you do when you really want to irritate a grown-up.

I didn't have to go far. My friend Richard Watson was nearby, and he shuffled along on the floor to make room for me. I sat down and watched as our captors separated, the witch heading for the doors, the vampire returning to her former position.

'Psst, Richard,' I whispered. 'What have you got on the horror-movie double act? Who are they, for heaven's sake?'

'I don't know, Sam,' he whispered back, his voice a touch shaky. 'One minute we were in class with Mrs Sternwood taking the register, the next we were being forced to come here.'

'What did they say?' I asked.

'Not a lot,' replied Richard. 'Just that no-one would get hurt if we co-operated. What do you reckon they're after, Sam?'

'Hard to tell, Richard,' I murmured. 'We'll have to . . .'

'Who's that talking?' shouted the vampire. 'It's you again, isn't it – Miss clever-clogs!' She pointed her gun at me. 'Now *this* is your last warning. Keep that big mouth of yours shut, and put your hands up like the others, or . . .'

'OK, OK, I get the picture,' I said, reaching for the sky. 'There's no need to make a big deal out of it.'

'How *dare* you speak to one of my pupils in that manner!' spluttered Mr Pinkerton suddenly. His bald head was shining and he looked positively furious. 'This is . . . an *outrage*. You can't just barge into my school and make threats like that. I simply won't have it, do you hear?'

Good for you, Mr Pinkerton, I

thought. You tell 'em!

'Zip it, Pinkerton, you old twit,' said the vampire. 'This will all be over soon, and you can go back to your office for a nice cup of tea and a couple of chocolate biscuits. And if you do as you're told, you won't find the tea running out through any nasty bullet holes . . . Understand?'

For a second I thought Mr Pinkerton was going to explode.

He didn't. He paused . . . then nodded instead. But I could tell he wasn't happy. He has very thick eyebrows, and they were squashed together at the top of his nose, which tends to be a rather bad sign. It always reminds me of those big black clouds that appear just before a storm.

It looked as if we were in for some pretty stormy weather, too, but not from Mr Pinkerton. A dark cloud was hanging over us, and it wasn't the kind that produces rain. This one meant trouble. If only I knew what these thugs were up to, I thought, then I might be able to stop them.

A tide of anger began to sweep through my mind. I absolutely *detest* being ordered around by adults as if I didn't matter. It's something they all do – parents, teachers, dinner ladies – and it can really get to me. But this was even worse. I was trapped, at the criminals' mercy . . .

Cool your jets, Marlowe, I said to myself. Easy does it. I took a deep breath, and let it out slowly. Losing my grip wouldn't help. I had been forbidden to speak, but I could still use my secret weapon – the skills of a brilliant girl detective. By staying alert I might work out what was in store.

I made a start by going over what our captors had said since I'd been nabbed. You won't be surprised to hear I didn't think they liked children much, especially me, and there had been something rather odd about the way the vampire had spoken to Mr Pinkerton, although I couldn't quite put my finger on it . . .

Neither of those things seemed to lead anywhere for the moment, so I tucked them into the To-Be-Investigated-Later section of my brain. I also filed away in there the fact that they'd been arguing. Then I scanned the hall, making sure the vampire and the witch didn't see what I was doing.

There wasn't much to go on. Some

of the younger kids were fidgeting like they were about to wet themselves. But they always do that in assembly. Most of the others looked pale and scared, and everyone was struggling to keep their arms up. My shoulders were aching now, too. I could take the pain, though.

I automatically made note of Steven Greenstreet's position. He's my deadliest enemy, and I like to keep track of where he is. His Royal Dimness was sitting a few metres away to my right, with the other four members of his gang. They're so incredibly terrifying I call them . . . *The Feeble Five*.

Near Greenstreet I could see Justin Thunder's fair hair and freckled features. That figured. Greenstreet specializes in crawling, and because Justin has a famous father, the creep hadn't left the poor boy alone all term. He was probably hoping to get his grubby paws into some of Mr Thunder's millions.

And that's it, I realized, suddenly. For a second I almost felt ashamed to call myself a detective. I wondered why I had been so stupid. A pair of pistol-packing baddies turn up on the morning a world-famous, fabulously rich rock star comes to my school, and it takes me *how* long to make the connection?

No Brownie points for you today, Marlowe.

This was obviously a kidnap caper, and Riff Thunder was the target. The question was – what could I do? I started thinking, fast. I needn't have bothered. I'd already run out of time.

'They're here,' said the vampire softly.

While I'd been concentrating on Greenstreet, she'd slipped over to the tall windows that overlooked the street, and had hidden behind a curtain. A ridiculously long car was pulling up at the gate. The boot seemed to arrive five minutes after the front bumper. So that's what a stretch limo is, I thought.

The chauffeur opened a rear door. Two men emerged and headed for the school. One was youngish and wearing a suit. His hair looked damp, as if he'd just washed it. The other was as old as my dad, but had long, blonde hair, and was sporting skin-tight leather jeans, a red satin bomber jacket and mirror shades.

There were no prizes for guessing who was the rock star.

'Not a word from *anybody*,' hissed the witch. The vampire ran across and joined her. They flattened themselves against the walls on either side of the doors, guns held high.

The tension was unbearable. I looked round desperately, and caught sight of Justin's white, frightened face. Our eyes locked, and in that instant I realized he knew the awful truth.

Then everything went into slow motion. The doors swung wide and Riff Thunder strolled in, smiling and waving. The witch jumped forward to grab him, the vampire threw something down, and evil-smelling smoke filled the hall. I leaped up . . .

But I was too late. Our captors had vanished.

And they had taken Riff Thunder with them.

Chapter Three

I was five metres from the hall doors, but it might as well have been five light years. I just couldn't get through the mob of struggling kids, some of whom were screaming their heads off. The others were too busy choking on the smoke.

I wasn't, mainly because I'd hit the pause button as far as breathing was concerned. One whiff had been plenty. It was the worst pong I'd ever had the bad luck to encounter.

'Don't panic, children!' shouted Mr Pinkerton above the din. 'Remember what we practised in our fire drills!'

Fat chance, I thought, as a knot of

bodies finally burst into the reception area, and I followed. I didn't hang around. I made straight for the playground. Outside I gulped in great mouthfuls of air, and scanned the street for a getaway car. But there was nothing, no speeding vehicle, no squeal of tyres.

I ran out of the gate and up to the stretch limo. The chauffeur was leaning against the bonnet, and looked startled as I skidded to a stop in front of him.

'Which way did they go?' I asked.

'Who?' he said, confused now.

'The kidna . . .' I started to say, but the words died on my tongue. He couldn't possibly have missed two armed villains in amazing disguises dragging off the star he'd just delivered. If they'd made their exit past him, that is. Which could only mean one thing. They hadn't. 'Oh, never mind,' I finished.

I dashed back to the school. Everyone else seemed to be in the playground now. The teachers were trying to get the milling, coughing crowd organized into classes, but they weren't having much success. I dodged past and slipped inside, ready to hold my breath again if necessary.

The hall doors were wide open, and little swirls of smoke drifted across the empty floor. The smell had faded, thank goodness, although the hint that was left frightened the wits out of my nose. It wrinkled up and did a lot of twitching as I made for the corridor I'd come down earlier.

'And where do you think you're off to, Samantha Marlowe?'

I stopped dead, then looked over my shoulder. Mrs Sternwood was standing in the doorway of Mrs Brown's office.

'I wanted to see if the kidnappers had escaped this way, Miss,' I said. 'I'm sure they didn't leave by the gate, and . . .'

'And *I'm* sure that's something we ought to let the police deal

37

with,' interrupted Mrs Sternwood. 'I've just called them, and they should be here at any minute. Meanwhile, young lady, you and I will join the others in the playground.'

'But Miss . . .' I started to cry.

I decided to give up on the rest of the sentence when I saw she was letting me have it with that well-known lethal weapon, The Sternwood Stare. It can reduce even the toughest kids to snivelling wrecks in seconds. It's also as good as a neon sign on her forehead flashing *Beware – Teacher On Overload*.

She was letting me have it with that well-known lethal weapon the Sternwood Stare.

Actually, I'm pretty immune to it. You would be too if you'd seen it as often as I have. But Mrs Sternwood is OK, and she had enough on her plate without me adding to it. So it was back to being a schoolgirl for a while, and I meekly followed her out into the playground. Not that I minded much.

I would be on top of this case soon enough. It was a question of pride. This was *my* patch, and I wasn't about to let a couple of lowlife rogues do what they pleased on it. I wouldn't be able to relax until I'd hunted them down like a bloodhound and brought the pair to justice. And freed Mr Thunder, of course.

I had to admit I was looking forward to the chase, though.

It was going to be a *lot* of fun.

Eventually, the teachers calmed down the mob in the playground, and got us as organized as they ever do. By the time the first police car came racing up to the gate, lights flashing and siren blaring, we were being hustled into school. From inside I heard more cars screeching to a stop on Chandler Street.

Mrs Sternwood told us to sit at our desks, but nobody took any notice. Instead, we piled over to the windows so we could watch. And what I saw was enough to make a young gumshoe's toes curl with pleasure. The boys in blue were everywhere. Several were trying to hold back a group of people at the gate.

'Wow!' said Richard, suddenly, his eyes popping. 'That's the lady from the TV news, isn't it?'

Well spotted, Richard, I thought. It *was* Connie Ross, the reporter who handles crime stories on the major network news show. I was impressed. She and her all-woman camera crew had made it to this particular scene incredibly fast. I wondered how she had found out about this morning's events so quickly.

'Cor, maybe she'll interview me,'

said Greenstreet. 'I've always wanted to be on TV.'

'Don't count on it,' I said. 'She doesn't do wildlife programmes. Besides, that series about gorillas is over.'

Everyone burst into laughter. Everyone, that is, except Greenstreet, who hunched his shoulders and scowled at me fiercely. He didn't seem to realize that made him even more like a gorilla than ever.

Actually, that's a bit unkind – to gorillas, that is. Most are much better looking than him.

'That kidnapper was right,' he snapped. 'You *are* a clever-clogs, and some day you'll be too clever for your own good.'

'At least I don't trail my knuckles on the ground when I walk,' I said, and smiled as the laughter doubled.

Greenstreet angrily thrust his hands deep into his trouser pockets, and gave me one of those I'll-Get-Even-With-You-Marlowe stares of his. I honestly can't understand why he bothers. They're like water off a detective's raincoat.

'OK, you two, that's enough of that,' said Mrs Sternwood. 'Now come along, Class Nine, I won't tell you again. I know this is all very thrilling, but you really must settle down.'

She stepped in to shoo us away from the windows, and within a few minutes we were sitting at our desks. But the classroom was still crackling with excitement. My schoolmates were talking at the tops of their voices about what had happened. It isn't every day they witness a celebrity kidnap, I suppose.

No-one seemed to be suffering any after-effects from the smoke in the hall, though. Mrs Sternwood went round the class checking we were OK, just to make sure.

'Do you think we'll be sent home, Miss?' asked Donna.

I certainly hope not, I thought. For once in my life the only place in the whole universe I wanted to be was at school. I had a feeling I'd get nowhere with this case unless I stayed here.

'I really don't know, Donna,' said Mrs Sternwood. 'Although I can't see us getting much work done today. Anyway, whatever Mr Pinkerton and the police decide, I still ought to finish taking the register . . . Which reminds me, Samantha,' she paused. 'Would you care to explain where *you* were earlier this morning?'

43

I'd been expecting that. I smiled, and trotted out my library excuse. I said I'd realized I'd missed registration, then hurried to the hall for assembly, only to discover the school day was getting off to a rather unusual start. Mrs Sternwood's expression told me she didn't buy all of my story.

But she bought enough to let me off the hook.

Of course, I had to put up with the inevitable lecture on the subject of my punctuality, complete with a new twist. Mrs Sternwood said I had been lucky not to get badly hurt, and that I'd put myself in real danger by not being in the right place. She seemed to forget that *everyone* had been at risk.

I didn't say that, though. As we all know, grown-ups hate being contradicted. Mrs Sternwood was just moving on to my other faults when the door opened and Mr Pinkerton hurried in.

'Ah, Mrs Starkey,' he said, breathlessly. Nobody's name is safe with Mr Pinkerton. He always gets them wrong. 'Wasn't it one of your girls who tangled with the intruders?'

'That's right, Mr Pinkerton,' said Mrs Sternwood. 'It was Samantha Marlowe.'

'Well, I wonder if I could borrow her for a while?' said Mr Pinkerton, peering at me from beneath his bushy eyebrows. They'd returned to their normal positions, one several centimetres higher than the other. 'The police think she might be able to, er . . . assist them with their enquiries.'

'Why, certainly,' said Mrs Sternwood. 'And make sure you do your best to be helpful, Samantha.'

I smiled so sweetly I was almost sick on the spot. I didn't look at the other kids as Mr Pinkerton and I left the classroom. But I could feel their stares boring into my back.

'This is all so distressing, *so* distressing,' Mr Pinkerton muttered as he strode down the corridor. I had to scamper to keep up with him. He swept past Mrs Brown, who smiled reassuringly at me, and into his office. It's quite small, and the four people waiting there made it seem crowded.

I realized straight off that two were police officers. One was in plain clothes, the same kind of dull, dark suit senior cops always wear, although the blue suede shoes and long sideburns were a little unusual. The other was a fresh-faced, uniformed constable with neat hair and large glasses. The third person was a pale, anxious-looking Justin Thunder.

The fourth was in the corner, speaking quietly into a mobile phone. I recognized him as the man who had followed Justin's dad out of the stretch limo and into the school.

'But . . . you can't be serious . . . no, wait!' he said, then lowered the phone. The conversation was obviously over.

'Was it them?' said the plain-clothes policeman.

'Yeah, and they've set the ransom for Riff,' said the man. 'They want . . . *one million pounds*!'

Chapter Four

'Well, bless my soul, they don't come cheap,' said the plain-clothes policeman. 'Not that it matters how much they're after. We never give in to ransom demands, do we, Constable Holly?'

'That'll be the day, Inspector Presley, sir,' said the constable, smiling broadly, hands behind his back.

'Now just a second there,' said the man with the mobile phone. He was very calm. 'Let's not be too hasty . . . I mean, this is your gig, Inspector, and I'm sure you guys know what you're doing. But it's Riff's safety I'm worried about, and those kidnappers sound pretty hard-boiled to me.'

'Are you saying we should give a million pounds to a couple of *criminals*?' Inspector Presley asked. He seemed shocked.

'No, I was thinking of using it as bait,' the man replied. 'They said they'd call later with details of when and how to pay. Couldn't you set up some kind of trap? That way we'd get Riff back, *and* you'd catch the kidnappers at the same time. Hey, what d'ya say, Inspector? Is that a neat plan, or *what*?'

'You know, I believe you might have something there,' said Inspector Presley. 'It would be highly irregular, but . . .'

I had been standing behind Mr Pinkerton during this exchange, ears on maximum alert and not daring to bat an eyelash. It was just the sort of top-notch information I needed, and I knew they'd clam up the instant they realized I was there.

Mr Pinkerton kept trying to interrupt, and finally made it.

'Ahem . . . ahem!' he coughed loudly at last, and moved aside. The conversation died as quickly as if someone had shot it. 'This is the girl you wanted to see, Inspector Pitney . . .'

Four pairs of eyes and one pair of lenses turned to me. This was obviously my day for being the centre of attention. That was fine – for the moment. I knew I might have to keep a low profile later on. But that wouldn't be difficult. I can make myself harder to spot than a shadow in an eclipse.

'The name's Presley, actually,' said the Inspector, giving me a big smile – the sort adults always put on when they want kids to think they're incredibly nice. Then his face changed and he tried to look sympathetic. 'And I hear you had a *nasty* encounter, young lady. It must have been so *horrible* for you.'

I nearly replied that it hadn't been as awful as listening to him talk to

me like I was a dim four-year-old. But I didn't.

'It wasn't that bad,' I said, shrugging and examining my fingernails. 'In fact, I've been more frightened by some of the school dinners I've seen in this place than by those two.'

'But how can you say such a thing, Sally?' spluttered Mr Pinkerton. 'Why, I was under the impression we were having much less trouble since we got rid of the last cook . . .'

'Perhaps that's a subject you could discuss at some other time, Mr Pinkerton,' said Inspector Presley. Then he flashed me that smile again. 'I think we have rather more pressing business. Now, my dear, I wonder if you could tell me what you remember about the incident? It might be *really* important . . .'

'I'd like to see some ID first,' I said. Inspector Presley's smile disappeared, and Mr Pinkerton's jaw dropped. 'After all, I know Mr Pinkerton and Justin.' I nodded to the latter, and he nodded in return. 'But I don't know the rest of you. And my mum's always told me I should never speak to strangers.'

'Er, quite right, too,' said Inspector Presley before Mr Pinkerton could recover. 'Your mother has a point . . .'

The two policemen dug in their pockets and produced their warrant cards. I examined them closely, trying not to laugh at the photographs, then looked expectantly at Mr Mobile Phone.

'Hi, the name's Jerry Sharp,' he said. 'I'm Riff's manager, and I want you to know it's a pleasure to meet you. I'm sure my pal Justin here will vouch for me . . .'

He held out his hand, and I noticed he was wearing the sort of gold watch I'd never be able to afford on my pocket money. His smile contained so many gleaming white teeth I was almost dazzled, and his hand-shake was dry and firm. But there was something about him that made me

feel uncomfortable enough to want to count my fingers when I got my hand back.

It could have been the way his eyes slid from my gaze. Or maybe it was because of Justin's reaction. Sure, he said the guy was OK. But as he did so, my schoolmate's face looked like mine probably does when I'm in the same room as Greenstreet.

Jerry Sharp was definitely a man to be watched.

'Right, do you think we could proceed?' said Inspector Presley, who seemed to be losing his patience.

'Hang on a minute,' I said. 'There's a question *I* want an answer to first. Why isn't this case being handled by Inspector Raven? This is his beat, isn't it?'

'It usually is,' said Inspector Presley, looking surprised. 'But when the call about the kidnap came in this morning he asked *me* to deal with it. He said something about not wanting to go anywhere near Chandler Street School ever again. He mentioned a name, too, I seem to recall. Now, what was it . . .'

'Sam Marlowe?' I said, and smiled.

'How on earth . . .' said Inspector Presley, puzzled. Then his face lit up with sudden realization. 'It's you, isn't it?'

Of course, the story of my previous dealings with Inspector Raven had to come out then. Inspector Presley listened as I went over the cases

I'd solved for his colleague. I was interested to hear that old Raven was getting soft. Still, if you can't stand the heat, stay out of the playground, that's what I always say.

Inspector Presley didn't even wait for me to finish before he launched into the usual stuff about how I was only a kid, and I shouldn't interfere in police business, and what ghastly punishments were in store for me if I did. It was tough listening to him. Tough listening without *yawning*, I mean.

'And let me hasten to add,' said a flustered Mr Pinkerton as soon as Inspector Presley drew breath, 'that the criminal activity young Sally described had absolutely *nothing* to do with Chandler Street Junior School, and furthermore . . .'

Inspector Presley shut him up with a look which was almost as powerful as The Sternwood Stare, then began rapidly firing questions at me. Constable Holly scribbled down my replies in a little notebook. The inspector was pretty slick at his job. Within a couple of minutes he'd winkled out of me what had happened, as well as full descriptions of the villains.

He wasn't quite slick enough, though.

I didn't mention the part about arriving late and using my secret entrance, or my suspicion that the kidnappers hadn't escaped through the main gate. I figured he'd be able to work that out when he questioned the chauffeur, or maybe Jerry Sharp. Although I didn't remember seeing him at the time . . .

Besides – it was a lead I might want to pursue myself.

'Well, I must admit you've been *very* co-operative, young lady,' said Inspector Presley, whose smile had returned. Mine hadn't. I was thinking of treading on his blue suede shoes for using those last two words. 'You can run along now. But just remember – behave yourself. Stick to your skipping, or whatever it is little girls do these days, and keep out of our way.'

With that, he turned round and started talking to Jerry Sharp as if I didn't exist. I clenched my teeth and narrowed my eyes . . . but then I calmed down. It didn't matter, I thought. I knew Inspector Presley would treat me a whole lot differently when I wrapped up this case for him. He'd have to.

As I was heading for the door, I heard Mr Pinkerton ask if Justin should go back to class too. Inspector Presley said that was the best idea for the time being. He also told Justin not to worry. They'd soon have his dad home and the kidnappers behind bars, where they belonged.

Judging by the expression on Justin's face when he emerged from Mr Pinkerton's office, he was having trouble believing either of those things. I waited for him to catch up with me in the corridor, and we walked together. But when we got to our classroom door, I grabbed his arm and dragged him past.

'Hey, what are you doing?' he said, resisting.

I put my finger to my lips and mimed 'Sssh!' Justin looked at me as if I'd gone totally bananas, then suddenly stopped struggling. A few seconds later we were in my favourite hideaway, the school library. I was positive no-one had seen us. I quietly eased the door shut, and turned to face him.

'I don't know what you're after,' he said wearily, as if he was resigned to his fate. 'But couldn't you just leave me alone? I can't get you any autographs or CDs or T-shirts at the moment, what with my dad being kidnapped and all.'

I didn't blame him for thinking I

was trying a shakedown. I'd seen enough of what he'd been through so far this term to have a rough idea of how he felt. Greenstreet hadn't been the only one to pester him. Lots of other kids had too, and even some of the teachers had asked him for concert tickets.

'Relax, Justin,' I said. 'That isn't why I brought you here.'

'So why *did* you, then?' he said, a puzzled expression on his face. He sighed, and leaned back against the sparsely occupied bookshelves. 'If you wanted to recommend a book, you really needn't have bothered. I don't mean to be ungrateful, but I'm not exactly in the mood for reading right now.'

'Actually, I was just going to ask you a simple question,' I said. 'Who do you reckon is more likely to find your dad and free him – a brilliant private detective who also happens to be an eleven-year-old schoolgirl, or those two bozos with big feet I was

60

talking to in Mr Pinkerton's office?'

Justin stared at me for an instant, his face blank. Then he grinned, and I knew I'd got through to him.

The old Marlowe charm had done it again.

Chapter Five

'Listen, I'm sorry I thought you were like everyone else,' said Justin. 'Sometimes it's an easy mistake to make.'

'No problem,' I said. 'I've had a fair amount of publicity myself in the past, so I know what it can do to people.'

'Then it's true,' he said, with more than a touch of admiration in his voice. 'I thought the other kids were just trying to wind me up when they went on about you catching some criminals and having your picture in the newspapers. But you can't *really* be a private detective, can you?'

'You better believe it, pal,' I said, proudly. 'I'm the best there is. I'm offering to take *you* on as my client, too, and just to show this has nothing to do with the size of your dad's bank balance, there's absolutely no charge. I've got reasons of my own for wanting to catch the duo that snatched him.'

'Thanks, but I'm not sure I should accept...' said Justin, doubtfully. 'Inspector Presley was dead set against you being involved, wasn't he? And he must know what he's doing.'

'Whatever he does, though, it won't include *you*,' I said. 'You'll have to sit on your rear end twiddling your thumbs while you wait for him to explain what's happening. But stick with me, kid, and I guarantee you'll be part of the action.'

'That would make a change . . .' said Justin, his face taking on a strange look. Then his grin made a comeback. 'OK, Sam,' he continued. 'I'll go for it. Where do we start?'

'Where all the great detectives start, Justin,' I said. 'With facts. Plenty of hard facts . . .'

What I didn't say was that something smelt funny in this caper, and it wasn't just the smoke that had nearly choked us in the hall. There was another whiff, one that only I could smell, and it made me want to dig up as much information on Mr Riff Thunder as I could. I didn't know why. But I've learned it pays to go with the flow in the early stages of a case.

Justin didn't need much prompting to talk about his dad and life as the son of a legendary rock star. To an outsider, someone thick like Greenstreet, for instance, it would have seemed incredibly glamorous. But I could see it might have had some disadvantages. In fact, Justin revealed there were plenty.

Sure, Riff was rich and had houses dotted round the world. But for Justin that only meant never staying in a place long enough to feel at

Justin didn't need much prompting to talk about his dad.

home. He'd gone to lots of expensive private schools, too, and had been treated the same in each one – as if he were nothing more than a stepping stone for getting closer to his father. Chandler Street had been no different.

Nobody realized that Justin himself didn't often get very close to his dad. Riff spent most of every year on tour, or in the recording studios.

Whole weeks went by when the only contact his son had with him was the occasional brief phone call from a hotel room or an airport. Charming, I thought.

'What about your mum?' I said. 'You haven't mentioned her.'

'She died in a car crash when I was little,' said Justin, quietly. 'I don't remember much about her. Dad's had loads of girlfriends since, but he's never wanted to marry any of them. There's always a housekeeper to take care of me while he's away. But they don't seem to last, either.'

I let him go on, and gradually a picture began to form in my mind. I saw Justin alone in a big house somewhere, watching TV, surrounded by the computer games and other gadgets his dad's money had bought. He didn't spell it out, but I guessed none of them made up for not having any proper friends.

Or a dad who wanted to be with you.

A couple of things seemed odd, though. If Riff was that rich, why did he work so hard? As far as I knew, rock stars with his sort of wealth seemed to be on holiday permanently – at least, when they weren't at wild parties, that is. But it sounded as if Riff was flogging himself half to death.

It didn't make sense, somehow. And neither did Justin's presence at Chandler Street Junior. It was the first school he'd been at where your parents didn't have to pay to get you in. Actually, if they could have, most of its current pupils would have paid to get out. But let's not go into that.

I asked Justin about both points, and his answers featured a single name – Jerry Sharp. Justin said he thought his dad had wanted to ease off a bit recently. He wasn't getting any younger, after all. But for some reason Jerry seemed determined to keep him on the road and churning out records. It had also been Jerry who'd suggested Justin come to Chandler Street.

'Did he explain why he thought it was a good idea?' I asked.

'Not exactly,' Justin replied. 'Although I did hear him talking to Dad about it being . . . convenient. Yes, that's the word he used. Is it important, Sam?'

'Probably not,' I said, quickly. I didn't want Justin jumping to any conclusions until I'd mulled over what he'd given me. He seemed anxious enough as it was. 'What do you think of Jerry?'

'I can't stand him,' said Justin, without hesitation. 'I mean, he's never been horrible to me or anything. It's just that whenever he's around he makes me feel . . .'

'Uncomfortable?' I said.

'That's right,' said Justin, impressed. 'How did you know?'

'All part of the job, Justin,' I said, zapping him with my There's - Nothing - We - Detectives - Can't - Do

68

smile. 'OK, you'd better get back to class. You can tell Mrs Sternwood the police reckon they won't be finished with me for ages yet. Now that's a story she *will* believe for once. I'll see you later.'

'What are you going to do?' he said as I opened the door and peered along the corridor. There was no-one in sight.

'I'm going to start tracking down your dad,' I said. But I stopped on the threshold. Something had occurred to me. 'One last question. You do *want* me to find him, don't you? He doesn't seem to have done much for you lately.'

'That may be so,' said Justin, with a shrug. Then he looked me straight in the eyes. 'But he's still my dad.'

He didn't have to say any more. As kids, we understood each other perfectly. Grown-ups, I thought. What a pain they are. Can't live with them, can't live without them . . .

Justin waited at Class Nine's door while I slipped past. I signalled as soon as I was safe, and he went in. Then I sped off towards the reception area.

I didn't have to worry too much about anybody spotting me, though. Mr Pinkerton had very handily ordered the teachers to make sure everybody stayed in class until he had worked out what to do. And knowing him, that could take some time. But I already had my next move mapped out.

For me to have any real chance of finding Justin's dad, I had to know what the kidnappers were saying. And somehow I had a feeling I wouldn't get the answer I wanted if I simply went up to Inspector Presley and asked him. Not even if I said *pretty please*, and did a curtsey. So I had to think of something else.

The solution had come to me in a flash. Or rather, a squawk.

Mr Pinkerton and Mrs Brown kept the door between their offices closed most of the time, and talked with each other through an intercom system. They each had a little black box on their desks they could speak into. Mr Pinkerton, however, didn't know that Mrs Brown regularly used *hers* to listen in on conversations he would rather have kept secret.

I'd discovered this last term on a day when I'd taken the register to the secretary's office. Mrs Brown had gone bright red when I'd walked in, and had swiftly silenced the squawking intercom with one jab of a plump finger. But it had been too late. I had recognized Mr Pinkerton's voice instantly. He had been moaning to somebody's parents about their son's behaviour.

With any luck, Inspector Presley, Constable Holly and Jerry Sharp would have remained in Mr Pinkerton's office to talk about the case. If

None of the cops heard my footsteps......

they had, I knew Mrs Brown wouldn't be able to resist the temptation to eavesdrop. It was bound to be more exciting than the stuff she usually heard, after all. And if she were listening in, I might as well, too.

I stopped at the end of the corridor and carefully spied out the land ahead. Across the reception area I could see the welcome banner was still in place. But now, instead of kids, teachers and masked villains, the hall was packed with policemen searching for evidence. A couple were dusting the open doors for finger-prints, their backs turned to me.

Time for that low profile, I thought, running quickly and softly in the direction of Mrs Brown's office. None of the cops heard my footsteps, or even caught a fleeting glimpse of me.

I ducked down behind the hot drinks dispenser next to Mrs Brown's door. It was pretty big, and similar to the kids of Chandler Street School –

it never worked if it could help it. I reckoned it would provide enough cover for me to do some intensive earwigging of my own without being noticed.

The office door wasn't a problem. Mrs Brown had been thoughtful enough to leave it open. She was sitting at her desk, hunched over and listening hard.

My luck had held, too. The police and Jerry Sharp hadn't left yet. I kept very still, and began to tune in to what was being said. I couldn't have arrived at a better moment.

Jerry Sharp seemed to be doing most of the talking, but that was no surprise. He was saying something about Riff's record company being willing to supply the ransom money, when suddenly I heard a chirrupping noise. I realized it must have been his mobile phone. There was some mumbling, then he spoke clearly.

'That was the kidnappers again,'

he said. 'They've set a deadline. We've got three hours to pay up – or it looks like it could be the final curtain for Riff . . .'

Chapter Six

Three hours didn't leave me long to crack this case, but I wasn't that worried. Time might be tight, but I had a hunch I wasn't far from a breakthrough. A major suspect had entered the frame, and whenever his name was mentioned, or I heard him speak, sirens started wailing in my brain.

I'm talking about Jerry Sharp, of course. I hadn't liked him from the instant we'd met, mostly because my instincts had told me not to. But nothing I'd heard since had made me want to change my mind. In fact, some of what I'd got from Justin had only increased my suspicions. A lot.

Although it was an unusual choice, Jerry had said Chandler Street School would be 'convenient'. But convenient for whom? It had certainly been just that for the kidnappers. They seemed to have known precisely when Riff would be here and, except for me arriving late, the snatch had gone very smoothly indeed.

I also had a few doubts about the way Jerry had acted afterwards. For example, I hadn't noticed him in the reception area or the playground, even though I'd been one of the first people to leave the hall. Which meant there were several minutes when I was unable to account for his whereabouts.

Then there was his performance in Mr Pinkerton's office. As I remembered, Jerry hadn't seemed terribly bothered about what had happened. He'd been very cool. Much *too* cool, if you ask me. Here was somebody whose employer had been grabbed by a couple of wild, gun-toting hoodlums, and what does he do?

He calmly suggests a scheme to trap them, as if he found himself in similar situations every day. He was just like those presenters on children's TV. You know the ones I mean. They're supposed to be making some crummy model out of old toilet roll tubes, but when they hit the crucial, tricky part, they whip out a completely finished version from under the counter.

I'd almost expected Jerry to say 'and here's a plan I made earlier'. The guy deserved an Oscar, at least.

What was he up to? Was he involved in the kidnap? But why? I was sure the managers of famous rock stars were nearly as rich as the people they worked for, so I didn't think it could be a question of money. But then maybe he was just greedy.

Though that didn't make much sense, either. It would be like killing the goose who lays the golden egg – or gold disc, I should say. He would have been safer continuing to take a slice of the enormous amounts of dough Riff's records must rake in. If Jerry *was* involved in a crime and got caught, he could end up singing *Jailhouse Rock* for quite a while.

It was a mystery all right, and I couldn't see to the bottom of it yet. But I did know one thing. Whatever the truth turned out to be, Jerry Sharp was in this right up to the knot in his brightly-coloured, expensive silk tie. And with me on the case, that might just as well have been a noose.

I crouched there for what seemed like ages, listening to the crackly voices coming through the intercom on Mrs Brown's desk. But I didn't discover much. The only hot news was that Inspector Presley had obviously agreed to try trapping the kidnappers. He and Jerry were discussing the plan.

'As you guys know, I'm seeing the President of Riff's record company at their bank in an hour,' Jerry was saying. 'I'll pick up the money, then bring it here. The kidnappers are going to contact me once more, with instructions for the handover. And as soon as we know where they want that to happen . . .'

'We can make arrangements to give them something of a surprise,' said Inspector Presley. He sounded very pleased with himself. He was probably already dreaming about being promoted to Chief Inspector. Or maybe even Superintendent. 'Excellent, excellent . . . don't let us detain you any further, Mr Sharp.'

Next I heard the noise of chairs being pushed back, and I realized the meeting was over. I peered carefully round the hot drinks dispenser, and saw Mrs Brown hastily jabbing at the intercom, which squawked. Mr Pinkerton's office door opened a split second later, and the head bustled out.

I saw him shoot Mrs Brown an extremely suspicious look. A crimson line advanced swiftly up her neck, then started the endless trek across her many chins. But Mr Pinkerton didn't get an opportunity to say anything. The others had emerged, and stood between him and his secretary.

A crimson line advanced swiftly up her neck...

'One last point, Mr Sharp,' said Inspector Presley. 'I'd be much happier if you would allow Constable Holly to accompany you to the bank, and on your return with the ransom.'

'Hey, great idea, Inspector,' said Jerry, switching on that whiter-than-white smile of his. 'And call me Jerry, will you?'

'Of course, er . . . Jerry,' said the Inspector. 'Could I also trouble you for the bank's address? I'd like to have some more officers there standing by. Better to be safe than sorry.'

'I couldn't agree more,' said Jerry, pulling something out of a side pocket in his jacket. At first I thought it was his mobile phone again. 'Yeah, here it is. The Metropolitan Bank, 33 Penny Lane. The manager's called Mr Lennon.'

I had worked out by now that it wasn't his phone, the top of which was poking up from his breast pocket. It was a small, computerized diary. I should have known immediately.

Richard's been waffling on for ages about how wonderful they are at storing all kinds of important, personal information, and how he'd give anything to spend five minutes playing with one.

I felt much the same, although Jerry Sharp's was the only diary I was interested in. And it wasn't the machine itself that fascinated me. Just the prospect of what it might reveal.

I couldn't take my eyes off it. I watched as Jerry went to slip the diary back in his pocket . . . then stopped. Mr Pinkerton had come bustling across to shake his hand, and instead of putting the diary away, or in his other hand, Jerry hurriedly plonked it on the corner of Mrs Brown's desk.

Mr Pinkerton was talking to Jerry very fast, and pumping his hand up and down at the same time. I heard the head start wittering on about being a huge fan of Riff's, and how dreadful he felt that the kidnap had happened at Chandler Street. Jerry's eyes glazed over, and it took him a while to get away.

And when he did . . . he had forgotten his diary, thanks to good old Mr Pinkerton's ability to bore anyone stupid. It was still sitting on Mrs Brown's desk as Jerry, the two policemen and Mr Pinkerton came out. I ducked down as they filed past.

Jerry left the school. I saw Connie Ross and her camera crew swarm round him as he headed towards the stretch limo. I couldn't hear what he was saying, but I thought he looked as if he was enjoying himself. The two policemen walked quickly into the hall, Mr Pinkerton trailing behind them.

Now was my chance. I breathed out, moved round the drinks dispenser, and strolled into Mrs Brown's office. She was reading a thick paperback, and about to bite into a big bar of chocolate. I was impressed by the speed with which she'd produced those items. She was startled by my sudden appearance.

'Oh, it's you, Samantha,' she said, hurriedly closing the book and dropping the chocolate in a drawer. Then she pulled a small hanky from her sleeve and dabbed at her forehead. 'I wish you'd knock before you waltz in. You gave me quite a turn.'

'Sorry, Miss,' I said, my I'm-So-

Cute-Don't-You-Wish-You-Were-My-Granny smile on full beam. Mrs Brown always falls for it like a ton of bricks, and this occasion was no exception.

'Don't worry, love,' she said, relaxing. 'I'm just a bit jumpy after all that upset we had this morning. It was awful, wasn't it? Criminals with guns running around the school – I don't know what the world's coming to. Although that vile smoke took me back a few years, I can tell you . . .'

'Did it?' I said, not paying much attention. I was too busy edging towards Jerry's diary. It lay where Mrs Brown couldn't see it, behind a great heap of unsorted files, reports and papers. Then something about what she'd just said struck me. 'You mean you've smelt something like that before?'

'Oh yes,' said Mrs Brown. 'When the Darren twins were here, years ago, they had a habit of letting stink bombs off in assembly. And I swear the smell was exactly the same. Shut the door, sweetie, and I'll tell you all about it . . .'

Chapter Seven

Forty minutes later, I emerged from Mrs Brown's office with three things I hadn't had when I'd gone in there. The first was Jerry Sharp's diary. The second was some extremely interesting information about a couple of people who had been pupils at my school years before I was born.

And the third was a headache. But then, I thought as I made my way to class, that was a small price to pay for what I'd found out. I was pretty sure I knew who the kidnappers were.

I'd managed to pocket the diary not long after Mrs Brown had clicked into memory mode. I couldn't have stopped her talking once she hit the groove. Not that I wanted to. As tales of the Darren twins' years at Chandler Street poured out of her, I had begun to realize I'd stumbled on a vital lead.

Karen and Sharon Darren had entered Chandler Street Junior the same term that Mr Pinkerton had become head, and Mrs Brown his secretary. The girls were identical twins, and they had been trouble from Day One. Double trouble, according to Mrs Brown, although she was trying not to smile as she said it.

They had specialized in mischievous practical jokes, and had made Mr Pinkerton's life a misery with their lethal, home-made stink bombs. The only activity they enjoyed was music. But the head had banned them from that after the Christmas Concert Caper, a scam involving itching powder and the school choir.

It sounded as if Chandler Street had been quite lively in the old days.

I almost wished I'd been there.

The Darren twins had left eventually, and moved on to secondary school. Mrs Brown said she'd heard one or two stories about the mischief they'd got up to there, but then she'd lost track of them. According to her, Karen and Sharon had never re-visited the scene of their earliest stunts.

And that's where I was certain she was wrong.

I was convinced the Darren twins – grown up, but just as wild as ever – had appeared at Chandler Street earlier that morning.

They had been the kidnappers.

Everything fitted. I'd noticed that the villains had argued with each other just like my brother does with me, so I reckoned they had to be related. They'd been the same height and build, as well. But the clue that had clinched it was what the criminal in the vampire mask had said to Mr Pinkerton.

She'd called him an 'old twit', which was a reasonably accurate description, I suppose, if a bit harsh. But then she'd referred to him going back to his office for 'a nice cup of tea and a couple of chocolate biscuits'. At the time, something in that remark had made my detective's antennae twitch like mad. But I hadn't been able to work out what it was.

Now I could. How would a complete stranger know the head was addicted to chocolate biscuits with his morning tea? A lucky guess, you might say. I didn't think so. It was the sort of knowledge only a former inmate of the school would have. Especially a girl who'd spent a lot of time in Mr Pinkerton's office, watching him munch his favourite brand of digestives.

Believe me, it's a sight you *never* forget.

What I didn't understand was why the Darren girls had turned to crime. From Mrs Brown's description, they had seemed like a pair of good-natured tearaways, not desperadoes . . . Suddenly someone jostled me from behind, and woke me up to my surroundings again. A boy was dashing down the corridor, and I noticed most of the classrooms nearby seemed deserted.

Except one, that is. I opened Class Nine's door . . . and walked straight into my second Sternwood Stare of the day. Only this time it was backed by about another thirty-five withering looks.

'Ah, the wanderer returns,' said Mrs Sternwood. 'So good of you to grace us with your presence, Samantha. Perhaps you'd like to explain to your classmates what kept you. I told them they couldn't go home until you returned and I ticked your name in the register. They seem to be feeling rather impatient . . .'

Mr Pinkerton, I discovered, had reached his decision while I'd been taking that trip down Memory Lane with Mrs Brown. He'd given the school the rest of the day off, and Class Nine had been in possession of that particular piece of news for the last half-hour. With Mrs Brown's door closed and her rambling on, I hadn't heard everyone else leaving.

No wonder most of my classmates were unhappy. I'm surprised they didn't lynch me on the spot.

'Didn't Justin tell you, Miss?' I said, brightly. 'I've been talking to Inspector Presley about the kidnap.'

'Really?' said Mrs Sternwood with a menacing smile. My heart sank. I knew instantly that somehow I'd given her the wrong answer. 'Would that be the same Inspector Presley who was with Mr Pinkerton when he came to the class? Or are there two?'

'Well . . .' I mumbled. I felt like a rabbit caught in the headlights of a looming juggernaut. 'What I meant was . . .'

'Don't bother, Samantha,' said Mrs Sternwood. She put a tick in the register, then slammed it shut. 'I don't think I could face yet another of your incredibly inventive stories at the moment. Besides, you've wasted enough of our time for one day. We can discuss this tomorrow. Class dismissed!'

I quickly moved aside as most of Class Nine made a break for freedom. Richard hung back, but then I'd expected him to. He's been my assistant in enough cases to know I'd probably want him in on this. I was worried, though, to see Justin being swept along in Mrs Sternwood's wake. He was an essential part of the investigation, and I needed him with me.

'Excuse me, Miss,' I said, stepping smartly in front of her. 'But where are you going with Justin?'

'The police haven't managed to contact his father's housekeeper yet, Samantha,' she said with a sigh. 'I'm taking him to room three, which is where we're looking after some of the younger children whose parents can't collect them until later, for one reason or another. Do you have any objections?'

'No, Miss,' I said, thinking fast. 'Now you mention it, *my* mum and dad will both still be at work too, and my brother won't be in the house, either. So could *I* stay at school?'

'Of course, Samantha,' said Mrs Sternwood, giving me the kind of smile she does when she's about to set us an impossibly hard maths problem. 'I'm sure I can find something to occupy that over-heated brain of yours for a few hours . . .'

'Actually, Miss,' I said, 'I'd rather go to the library, if that's OK with you. There's such a lot to sort out . . . Wait a second! Could Justin help? He told me the other day he'd like to be a library monitor. Didn't you, Justin?'

'I did?' said Justin, startled. I turned away from Mrs Sternwood and kept winking at him until the penny dropped. 'Er . . . yes, that's right, Miss,' he continued.

Mrs Sternwood didn't reply. She looked at us searchingly instead. I could sense she wasn't keen on the idea. But I was ready for that. I knew how to swing things in my favour.

'Please, Miss,' I said. 'Justin's worried about his dad, and I think he could do with some peace and quiet. The library will be better for him than a classroom full of little kids.'

'Oh, very well,' said Mrs Sternwood. 'But you're both to stay there, do you hear?' We nodded. 'I shall check on you from time to time to make sure you're all right, and also to satisfy myself that you're not doing anything you shouldn't. I hope you won't give me cause to regret this, Samantha.'

'I won't, Miss,' I said, fingers crossed behind my back. Mrs Sternwood strode off, and I headed towards the library with Richard and Justin. But I had one more problem to deal with.

'Hey, Marlowe,' said a familiar,

'Hey Marlowe,' said a familiar unwelcome voice ....

unwelcome voice as we walked by the cloakroom. Greenstreet and his gang spread across the corridor in front of us like an unpleasant stain. 'Me and the lads wanted to have a word with you.'

'Fine, Greenstreet,' I said, pushing past him. 'Only just make sure that the word is . . . goodbye.'

'Ha *ha*, that's *really* funny,' said Greenstreet, trying to look tough, and failing. 'Excuse me while I die laughing.'

'Go on, then,' I said. Richard and Justin sniggered.

'OK, Marlowe, have your fun,' growled Greenstreet, scowling. 'But all I've got to say is this. If I've missed my chance to be on TV because you didn't come back to class on time, the joke's going to be . . . on . . . *you*.' He punctuated the last three words by poking a grubby, pudgy finger into my shoulder.

'Is that so?' I said, keeping my cool. 'Well, just remember I'm good at telling jokes, too – especially the *punch* lines.'

'Er . . . you don't scare me,' said Greenstreet, backing off. 'Come on, lads, let's go swimming. And I don't want to see you anywhere near the leisure centre, Marlowe. Understand?'

'I don't take orders from you, Greenstreet,' I said, and led my friends away without looking back.

He didn't worry me. I had more important things on my mind, anyway, like filling in some background for Richard when we got to the library. He listened as I went through what Justin had told me. I also revealed my theory about Jerry Sharp being part of the scam. Justin said he could believe it.

Then I dropped the bombshell about the Darren twins.

'You mean the kidnappers were once pupils at *this* school?' said Justin. Richard didn't speak, but I noticed his face had taken on an odd expression. 'That's incredible, Sam.'

'My thoughts exactly, Justin,' I said. 'But discovering *who* they are doesn't add up to much. It's *where* they are that really matters. If I knew that, I bet I could find your dad.'

'I might be able to help you there,'

said Richard, an edge of excitement in his voice. 'The Darren twins run the mini-market on the corner of Leonard Road . . .'

Chapter Eight

When my dad's surprised by something, like me getting a halfway decent school report, for example, he always says you could knock him down with a feather. Well, in the electrified silence which followed Richard's announcement, you wouldn't have needed anything that heavy to flatten me. Justin was gobsmacked too.

'Are you sure, Richard?' I asked at last.

'Absolutely positive,' he replied. 'My mum was at Chandler Street, and in the same class as the Darren girls, so I've heard all about them.

They turned up again last year. Mum recognized them straightaway when she went in the mini-market.'

I don't visit the place much, and as far as I remembered, I'd only ever seen one person behind the cash till. It hadn't occurred to me the shop might have been taken over by identical twins. Now I realized it was the perfect place for a pair of villains plotting to kidnap someone from our school.

'Brilliant, Richard,' I said, patting him on the shoulder. He looked as pleased as a dog that's finally managed to pass its stick-fetching exam. 'That could be the most important piece of information you've ever given me. And as a reward, I've got a job for you. I think you're going to enjoy this . . .'

I pulled Jerry Sharp's computerized diary out of my pocket. I explained who it belonged to, and how I'd come by it. Then I handed it over to Richard. His eyes lit up, and if

I handed it over to Richard. His eyes lit up....

he'd had a tail he would have been wagging it fit to bust. For a second I honestly thought he was going to start running around barking, he was so thrilled. He didn't. But it was close.

'Oh *wow*,' he said, breathlessly. 'A QX 1400! You wouldn't *believe* the capacity in this little marvel. It can . . .'

'Sorry, Richard,' I said. 'I don't mean to be a party pooper, but I haven't got time for the sales pitch. I just want to find out what that machine can tell us about Jerry Sharp.'

'That might be hard,' said Richard, frowning. 'You need a code word or phrase before you can access the data.'

'Can I help?' said Justin. 'We might have more luck if we work on it together. Besides, I've played with one of these things before, and I know Jerry better than you . . .'

Soon they were deeply enmeshed in a world of their own, one whose language they both spoke fluently. I saw that this could be the beginning of a beautiful friendship. So I felt it was best to leave them doing what they were good at, while I did the same. I had another important lead to check out.

'I'll be back in ten minutes,' I said, gently opening the door. Neither Richard nor Justin looked up from the diary, which they'd already persuaded to do some bleeping. 'If Mrs Sternwood comes snooping, tell her I'm in the loo.'

I didn't wait for an answer, and stepped into the corridor once more. I seemed to have spent the entire day creeping along it in one direction or another. But this time I only had to make a short dash to the rear of the building. Then I shot out of the school and across to the boiler house.

I reached it without any trouble. From there I slipped into the alley between the wall and the back of the bike sheds, and headed for my secret entrance. The late morning sky had clouded over, and darkness had seeped into the narrow space. There was still enough light for me to see something had changed, though.

I had left the door shut. Now it was open.

I paused, and carefully peered round it. There was no-one in the alley that led to Leonard Road, not that I'd expected there to be. I looked down, and just then the sun must have poked through a gap in the cloud. A golden ray appeared from above and struck a small object lying on the dead leaves a metre or so in front of me. It sparkled, and I pounced.

It was a pair of mirror shades, last seen earlier that day perched on the nose of a certain famous rock star.

I pounced. It was a pair of mirror shades.

I stood holding them in my hand, taking a moment to enjoy that delicious feeling I get when a lead turns into evidence. I'd been right. The kidnappers hadn't escaped through the main gate. They'd used an exit from the school I thought only I had known about. Which meant *they* had known about it too.

And that was more evidence against the Darren girls.

Several of the buildings that kept the ancient door hidden hadn't existed when the Darren twins had done their stretch at Chandler Street. Even if they had, somehow I reckoned Karen and Sharon had been the kind of kids who would have found a safe escape route. Knowing what they'd done to Mr Pinkerton, their survival had probably depended on it.

I could see the whole job now, almost as if I'd been there to catch it on film. The Darren twins sneaking into the school through my secret entrance, shutting the door behind them. Me coming through the door later, unaware of what was going on. Me being grabbed, the wait, the snatch, the confusion . . .

The Darren girls must have dragged Riff down the corridor, out past the boiler house and into the alley behind the bike sheds. I'd bet it had been difficult to get him through the door, especially if he'd been struggling. Which explained why they hadn't shut it, and also how he'd lost his shades.

Their destination had been, of course, the mini-market on the corner of Leonard Road. For the briefest of instants I was tempted to go there. But then I realized it probably wouldn't have been a bright move. If that's where they were holding Riff, a private eye barging in and asking a lot of questions might simply spook them into doing something stupid.

I'd be much better off going back to see what my two trusty assistants had come up with. My instincts told me that Jerry and the Darren twins were in cahoots. But so far I had nothing that connected them, or even that told me why Jerry might be involved in Riff's kidnap. I glanced at my watch.

I needed some proof. And I needed it *pronto*.

I pushed the door shut again, popped the shades into my pocket, and headed back to the library at the double. Richard was alone. He told me that Mrs Sternwood had turned up a couple of minutes before, and taken Justin to Mr Pinkerton's office. Inspector Presley had wanted to see him. Richard had managed to conceal the diary from Mrs Sternwood, though.

'Did you have time to find anything in it?' I said.

'You bet we did,' said Richard, grinning. 'Actually, I think we've solved the case for you. Justin was amazing. He cracked the entry code on his first go.'

'What was it?' I asked, curious.

'Number One,' replied Richard. 'Justin said it was obvious when you knew how Jerry's mind worked. And once we had access, getting the rest out of the memory was a piece of cake. Justin's really nice, Sam. We make an incredible team.'

'I'm very glad for you, Richard,' I said, and smiled. I was pleased to see him so happy. He looked like a puppy who's been allowed to play in a graveyard. I soon discovered he and Justin had dug up some juicy bones from Jerry Sharp's diary, too.

Enough to make a skeleton in a cupboard, in fact.

Richard pressed some buttons, and a stream of information began to appear on the little strip screen at the top of the QX 1400. He had been right about its capacity. It *did* contain a lot, including a list of phone numbers which featured Connie Ross's, among many others. Ah ha, I thought, especially when I saw the electronic asterisk blinking next to her name.

After that there were apparently endless lines of figures. At first I couldn't tell what they meant, but then suddenly it clicked. I was looking at details of money coming and going in various bank accounts that belonged to Jerry. Ah ha, I thought again. Riff's royalties provided the cash, but much more seemed to have been going *out* of Jerry's accounts than coming *in*.

Then we moved on to the diary part itself. It provided several riveting revelations. A date last week had a note reminding Jerry to pick up a plane ticket in the name of a Mr Jackson for a flight to Mexico, departing later . . . *today*. Oddly enough, the same Mr Jackson was due to visit a plastic surgery clinic in the Mexican city of Acapulco . . . *tomorrow*.

Finally something flashed past on the tiny screen that made me think 'ah ha' for the last time. It was the link I had been after. The date was just over a month ago. Jerry had booked a ten o'clock appointment with two people whose names had become very familiar to me in the last hour or so.

Karen and Sharon Darren.

'See what I mean?' said Richard, his grin getting bigger by the second. 'It's all there, isn't it?'

'Almost, Richard,' I said. 'But not quite.'

Most of the facts did sing out, and the song they sung was in a melancholy, minor key. It looked like Jerry's motive *had* been money. I guessed he'd lost his own, and a large amount of Riff's, in dodgy, perhaps illegal deals. From what I'd seen of his bank accounts, Jerry Sharp was flat broke, and had some major debts. No wonder he'd kept Riff working so hard.

Instead of coming clean, though, he'd hooked up with the Darren twins and devised a plot to kidnap Riff. Jerry intended to escape with his share of the ransom to Mexico, and adopt a new identity. So he got

Justin into Chandler Street, and the rest was history. But how did he plan to make his getaway?

Suddenly I heard footsteps approaching fast in the corridor. The door opened before I had time to do anything, although there was no cause for alarm. It was Justin, and I was relieved to see that Mrs Sternwood wasn't with him. But then I noticed the anxious look on his face, and felt uneasy. Very uneasy.

'What's happening, Justin?' I asked.

'Quick, Sam!' he replied. 'Jerry's had the call from the kidnappers, and he's left with the ransom to meet them . . .'

Chapter Nine

It was the kind of news I could have done without. Whatever Jerry's plan was, I knew he'd just taken the stage for the grand finale. This was definitely the beginning of the end, and unless I could work out some means of stopping him, he'd probably be well on his way to Mexico by tea-time.

He wouldn't be coming back for an encore, either.

Justin was still talking like a tape on fast forward, trying to convince me we ought to spill the beans to Inspector Presley immediately, or maybe even sooner. And Richard is very excitable, like most boys, so he

They managed to make the library seem even smaller than it was.

joined in, too. They managed to make the library seem even smaller than it was.

'OK, OK, you two,' I said eventually in the sort of loud, firm voice Mrs Sternwood puts on when Class Nine is getting out of hand. 'I think we all need to calm down. We won't be much use if we panic, will we?' They both went quiet. 'That's better. Right, Justin, tell me what's been happening.'

Justin took a deep breath, then rattled off what he'd discovered in Mr Pinkerton's office. Inspector Presley and Constable Holly had been waiting when he got there, along with Jerry, who had a briefcase containing the ransom. Jerry's phone had chirrupped, and he'd said it was the kidnappers. He claimed they told him it was time to meet them with the money.

Justin had asked where the meeting would be, but Inspector Presley said it wasn't something 'a little boy' needed to know. That sounded like a grown-up, I thought. If there's one thing adults love, it's keeping secrets from kids, especially when they involve serious stuff that affects us. I already knew the inspector hadn't got a clue about children's feelings.

'Did Jerry say anything else?' I asked.

'I don't think so,' said Justin, his brows furrowed. 'Constable Holly did, though. Inspector Presley asked him

116

if there'd been any problems, and Holly said no, not even when they'd stopped at the leisure centre on the return journey from the bank. Inspector Presley wasn't very happy about that, but Jerry said he'd had to collect something there.'

Apparently Jerry had been for a swim early this morning, before he'd picked Riff up and come to Chandler Street. That would explain why his hair had looked damp, I thought. He said he'd forgotten to put his watch back on, and that it must be in the changing-room locker. Constable Holly had waited outside, and Jerry had been gone for no more than a couple of minutes.

That seemed like an odd thing to do in the middle of all this, I thought. Was it part of Jerry's plan, I wondered? Holly said Jerry had taken the briefcase with him into the leisure centre. It *was* chained to his wrist, after all. Jerry had the key, but he'd had the briefcase when he'd emerged, and Justin, of course, had seen it in Mr Pinkerton's office.

Jerry's diversion nagged at me, but I couldn't work out where it fitted in. And I didn't have time to think about it any more. For Jerry had left with the police to help set up the trap for the kidnappers. At least, that's what he'd said he was going to do. I reckoned he had something else in mind.

I just didn't know what.

'*Please*, Sam,' said Richard, eagerly. 'Can we tell Inspector Presley now? Then he can arrest Jerry, and we'll be heroes!'

'Nice idea, Richard,' I said. 'But it's got a few holes in it. For a start, we don't even know where the inspector is, and I doubt if the police station would put us in touch with him. Besides, he wouldn't believe three schoolkids if they told him his hair was on fire and he could smell burning.'

'But couldn't we show him Jerry's diary?' asked Justin.

'We could, I suppose,' I said. 'But somehow I don't fancy trying to explain how it came to be in my possession. Anyway, I don't expect Inspector Presley would even look at it. He'd just hand it over to Jerry, who'd say thanks very much and make for the airport. Meanwhile I'd be staring at a theft rap.'

'So what *are* we going to do?' said Justin, his voice rising. He had the same worried expression on his face I remembered seeing in the seconds before his dad was grabbed.

'Take it easy, partner,' I said. 'We're not beaten yet. Jerry might be out of our reach, but the Darren twins aren't. If we can prove they're holding your dad at the mini-market, the police will *have* to believe us. Then there will be no hiding place for Jerry in Mexico, not even behind a new face. Let's hit the road, boys!

There isn't a second to lose!'

I dashed out of the library and headed for my secret entrance, with Richard and Justin following. They were utterly bewildered as I led them through, and pestered me with questions. I promised to explain about the door later. They still looked confused when we arrived at the mini-market.

I peered through the glass door, making sure I wasn't seen. The shop was empty except for one lone woman at the cash till. She had short, dark

hair, and she wasn't wearing a mask. But otherwise she was a dead ringer for either of the kidnappers. That was a good start, I thought. I'd gambled on the Darren twins being there, and we'd found one of them straightaway.

I sent Richard in first. Whichever Darren twin it might be, his role was to keep her occupied while Justin and I slipped into the shop unnoticed. Richard had suggested asking for a computer magazine from a shelf behind the counter, which he did. The Darren twin turned, and by the time she turned again, Justin and I were inside, concealed by a display of toys.

'Actually, this isn't the magazine I wanted,' I heard Richard say. I peeked, and saw the Darren twin give him an unpleasant look. 'It was *that* one, up there on the shelf above, with the picture of the robot on the cover.'

'What did *your* last slave die of?' said the Darren twin.

Now it dawned on me why the

Darrens didn't like kids much. It was because the shop they ran was near my school. Which meant that every afternoon at three-thirty, a horde of badly behaved, chocolate-crazed children descended on the mini-market to wreak total havoc. A year of that was bound to transform even the mildest-mannered shopkeeper into a Mrs Grumpy.

Then Justin nudged me and pointed at the display that was hiding us. It was a practical joker's dream, with phials of false blood, packets of itching powder, plastic tarantulas, and lots more. There was a Halloween section too, which included a couple of vampire and witch masks I'd seen before.

Last but not least, there were also some toy guns realistic enough to fool a whole school – *and* a certain girl detective.

I felt slightly cross with myself for not spotting the guns had been fakes. But I had to smile. I couldn't help admiring the way the Darren twins had pulled their most spectacular prank. It must have taken loads of guts, and that's something not everyone has got. It was just a shame I was on the right side of the law, and they were on the other. The wrong side.

None of that added up to the sort of proof I needed for Inspector Presley, though. I looked round, and saw a door in the corner. I signalled to Justin, and we scooted over to it, crouching down so we couldn't be seen. But Richard was doing his stuff. He'd asked for a third magazine, and the Darren twin's angry attention was entirely focused on him.

I couldn't stop to worry about Richard, though, not with the seconds ticking remorselessly by. The door appeared to be unlocked. I gingerly pushed it, and discovered a dark, dusty staircase. Justin and I climbed it quickly and silently. At the top was a landing with two more doors. We looked at each other. There was nothing for it. I'd have to dip.

'Eeny, meeny, miny, mo,' I whispered. 'Catch a villain by his toe. If he hollers, don't let go, eeny, meeny, miny mo!'

It was the one on the left. I gripped the handle, turned it, and eased the door open, revealing a room heaped with crates. The curtains were drawn across the window in the far wall. Lying on the floor was someone with his hands and feet tied, and a brown paper bag over his head. A man wearing a red satin bomber jacket and skin-tight leather jeans.

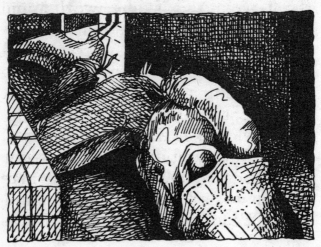

My brilliant detecting had led us to
. . . Riff Thunder!

'Dad!' said Justin, running in and
pulling off the bag.

'Justin!' said Riff, amazed.

Justin hugged his dad, and I think
father and son even shed a few tears.
I let them enjoy their reunion for a
while. But I knew I couldn't allow it
to go on very long.

'It's time we got you out of here,
Mr Thunder,' I said, walking over
to them. 'Help me with these ropes,
Justin.'

As we struggled with the knots, I
explained to Riff how we'd found
him. At last he was free, and stood
unsteadily, rubbing his wrists. I gave
him his shades, which he returned to
their perch on his nose. Then he put
an arm round Justin's shoulders.

'This totally freaks me out, Justin,'
he said, smiling and talking slowly.
'I mean, you and your friend here
coming to save me from those kidnappers. You know, I thought I was

on my way to rock and roll heaven when they grabbed me.'

'I don't like to hurry you, Mr Thunder,' I said, 'but . . .'

'I'll tell you something else, too,' he continued, completely ignoring me. Justin was looking at his dad, his eyes glistening as he listened. 'I've been lying there thinking about things . . . and I realized I haven't been much of a dad to you lately.'

I give up, I thought, and sat on a crate. Neither of them was going anywhere until Riff had said his piece. I had a nasty feeling his audience was about to get bigger, too.

Suddenly the door banged back, and Richard was shoved into the room. The Darren twins marched in behind him, then stood staring at Riff, Justin and me.

They didn't look too friendly, either.

Chapter Ten

'I'm sorry, Sam,' said Richard. 'She got suspicious, and took me to her sister in that room across the landing . . .'

'What are you kids doing here?' said one of the Darren twins crossly. 'This is private property. I've a good mind to . . .'

'Call the police?' I said. 'Don't let me stop you. I'd love to hear you explain how a famous, kidnapped rock star came to be lying tied up on your floor with a bag over his head.'

'Listen,' said the other twin. The two of them glanced at each other uneasily. 'This isn't the way it seems. That's the truth, isn't it, Mr Thunder? Can we tell her now?'

'Tell me what?' I said, turning to Riff.

'Don't ask me,' he said, shrugging. 'I've met disc jockeys who make more sense than they do. They're totally *crazy*.'

'Over to you, girls,' I said, turning back to them.

'Well, I don't suppose it'll do any harm,' said the same twin. 'We're not *really* kidnappers. This is a publicity stunt.'

And surprise, surprise, the person who had cooked it up was none other than Mr Oh-So-Slippery himself . . . Jerry Sharp.

According to Karen, who was the twin on the right, they had been trying to break into the music business ever since they'd left secondary school. At last they'd met Jerry, and he'd said he would give them jobs as backing singers in Riff's band . . . but only if they helped him with 'a special project'.

Riff's latest single was, of course,

Prisoner Of Your Love, and Jerry had suggested staging a fake kidnap. It was the kind of thing people in the music business did all the time, and the publicity ought to guarantee the song a number one spot. Or so Jerry had said. He'd also hinted it would do wonders for Karen's and Sharon's career. They'd jumped at the chance.

Sharon said they'd suggested Chandler Street School as the best place for the snatch because of the secret entrance and its nearness to the mini-market. But I got the impression they'd been looking forward to the prospect of playing one final, spectacular trick on Mr Pinkerton. Maybe they thought they'd have made it by now if he hadn't banned them from music.

'I'll take your word for it you're not a pair of thugs, and that you *thought* it was a stunt,' I said. 'But why did you tie Mr Thunder up? I mean, surely you didn't need to if it was for the publicity. Wouldn't he have known all about it?'

'Er . . . we thought he *did*,' mumbled Karen. She and her sister were both beginning to look embarrassed and uncomfortable. 'Mr Sharp said we had to make everything seem as authentic as possible, and that Riff would play along. He was going to struggle and complain a lot, and we were to take no notice.'

'We did think it was strange he kept it up even when we got back here,' added Sharon. 'Then we turned on the TV in the other room and saw the news reports. Just like Mr Sharp said we would. We phoned him when we were supposed to, and he said he'd bring the TV crew here later. He's due now, actually . . .'

Her voice trailed away. The Darren twins shifted from foot to foot in front of me, trying to smile, and looking like a couple of little kids who know they're in deep, deep trouble but can't understand why. I couldn't be too hard on the pair. It's tough seeing straight with stars in your eyes. They didn't seem to have a lot going for them in the brain department, either.

My mind was doing its job, though. It was sorting through the case for one last time, fitting the new information into a picture which was almost complete. Only one item was missing. I still didn't know how Jerry planned to get away with it. At this very moment he was out there somewhere with the ransom – but with dozens of police officers as well.

He'd even made sure a TV crew would be in the area. I reckoned he'd made an anonymous call to Connie Ross on his mobile phone when he'd disappeared after the kidnap, probably from an empty classroom. He'd needed her there to make the publicity angle look as if it was for real. And the Darren girls had fallen for it, being identical twin dimbos.

Hold on a second, I thought, suddenly. Perhaps I was staring the solution to the final puzzle in the face.

Or rather, two identical faces.

Looking at the twins made me realize *other* things could have doubles, too. What if Jerry had planted an empty briefcase at the leisure centre on his trip there early this morning? A briefcase that was exactly the same as the one he'd taken to the bank when he'd gone to collect the ransom money?

That was it, I thought, remembering that I'd noticed his watch when I'd first met him. *He hadn't left it behind at all!* His diversion on the way back from the bank had allowed him to pull the old switcheroo. The briefcase he had with him at the moment contained about as much as the Darren twins' heads.

I'd stake five years' pocket money on the ransom being in a locker at the leisure centre. I was certain Jerry intended to pick it up and vanish while the police were waiting to trap the kidnappers. Knowing the cops, they wouldn't want him hanging around when they thought something dangerous might happen.

Not that anything was going to. The police were in for a long, boring wait, and by the time they woke up, Jerry would be thousands of miles away. He had been fiendishly clever.

In fact, *he* was the one who had been too clever for his own good. His plan was brilliant, but he should have realized it was so complicated a single mistake might make it collapse like a house of cards. And leaving his diary on Mrs Brown's desk had been quite some error, particularly with me on the case.

As I said, when it comes to plans, simple is *always* best.

'Are you OK, Sam?' said Richard. 'You've gone very quiet.'

'I'm fine,' I replied. 'But two of the people in this room might feel a bit sick after they've heard what

I'm about to say. It looks to me like there's been a double-cross . . .'

I gave the Darren twins the works – Jerry's money troubles, how he'd tricked them, his ticket to Mexico and a new identity. They didn't want to believe me, but as I went through the whole caper piece by piece they began to look depressed. At one stage I thought they might even start blubbering.

'Does this mean they'll send us . . . to jail?' said Karen, reaching out for her sister's hand. They were both very pale.

'It might not come to that,' I said, re-assuringly. 'I'll put in a good word for you, and you can always tell the police you were conned. Although that will only work if we catch Jerry.'

'But that's impossible, isn't it, Sam?' asked Justin. 'You said yourself we don't even know where he is.'

'Ah, but I'm pretty sure I *do* now.' I quickly explained my theory about where Jerry had stashed the ransom money. 'And if my calculations are accurate,' I said, checking my watch, 'he's got to pick up the cash in the next ten minutes, or he won't have time to reach the airport for his flight to Mexico. We could still stop him at the leisure centre.'

'Well, what are we all waiting for?' chorused the Darren twins. 'We've got a car that'll get us there!'

Normally, there's no way I'd get in a car with two adults I didn't really know. But this was an emergency, and we did have another adult with us. Not much of an adult, but he'd do for now.

The Darren girls rushed downstairs and I went after them, with Richard, Justin and Riff close behind. The Darren twins' car was parked in the street outside, and if I'd needed any more evidence that they didn't have much between their ears, it would have been perfect. The car was a bright red sports model. Fitting two people in it would have been a tight squeeze, let alone six.

'Hey, welcome to problem city, people!' said Riff.

I didn't reply, for at that moment a van came round the corner and screeched to a halt at the kerb. Someone I recognized instantly leaned out. It was Connie Ross.

'What the . . . but isn't that . . .' she stammered. A camera woman began filming us over her shoulder.

'That's right, it *is* Riff Thunder,' I said. 'And this is the biggest scoop of your life. But I could make it even bigger if you take us to the leisure centre. Is it a deal?'

'You bet!' she said, grinning. 'Hop in!'

Richard, Justin, Riff and I piled into the van, and we shot off, the Darren twins following in their car. I outlined the whole case briefly for Connie Ross, and she said she'd known something was going on when the police had left the school. She and

We beat them to the leisure
Centre though.

her camera crew had been trying to find them.

And by a stroke of luck, that's exactly what we did.

As we squealed round a bend, I saw some familiar sideburns pop up from behind a hedge. A briefcase stood in a nearby phone booth, and I realized we had discovered the police trap. There was no sign of Jerry. He had obviously already slipped away. The boys, Riff and I waved at an utterly amazed Inspector Presley as we roared by. Seconds later I heard sirens wailing.

We beat them to the leisure centre, though. The stretch limo was in the car park, but I didn't say hello to the chauffeur. We ran directly to the changing rooms. We burst in . . . and there was Jerry Sharp, easing a bulging briefcase out of a locker. Before I could do anything, the Darren twins rushed across and leaped on him. He crashed into the door of a cubicle . . .

Which flew open to reveal a hideous

... which flew open to reveal a hideous sight....

sight – a naked, and very surprised Greenstreet! Richard and Justin fell about laughing, but Connie Ross's camera woman kept filming. She must have a strong stomach, I thought. Then maybe she'd done horror movies.

'Smile, Greenstreet,' I called out as the police arrived and started trying to separate a battered Jerry from his angry attackers. 'I mean, you did *want* to be on TV, didn't you?'

He gave me the old gorilla scowl and shook his fist.

Oh well, I thought. I've reunited a father and son, solved a major crime, caught an incredibly devious villain, and saved someone a lot of money. All before lunch, too. But then that's just another morning's work for Sam the Girl Detective.

And you can't please everyone, I suppose!

THE END

SAM, THE GIRL DETECTIVE

The Secret of the Seventh Candle

by Tony Bradman

There was a mystery waiting to be solved, and I knew only one person capable of doing it. Me.

A pair of bank robbers who seemed to vanish into thin air. A stately home, a lucky number – and a vicar with a vital clue. It starts with a school project, and suddenly Sam is up to her neck in a dramatic new mystery. Can she track down the villains and crack a case that has baffled the police for months? She has only a week in which to put all the pieces together . . .

The fourth title in a series of hilarious detective mysteries starring Sam Marlowe, intrepid girl detective.

0 440 86309 0

A SELECTED LIST OF TITLES AVAILABLE FROM YEARLING BOOKS